Do You Want to DANCE?

Dear Reader

Do you like to dance? Many people would answer "YES!" Whether you create your own dance, join in the latest dance craze or perform in a dance genre like ballet, it's important that you have fun!

Dance unites audiences in the universal language of movement, no matter where they live. In this book, we showcase different dances and dance companies from around the world. In Chapter 4 you'll find out about the AXIS Dance Company in the USA, whose dancers use wheelchairs in creative ways to present stunning stories through dance. And, in the final chapter, your eyes will light up when you see Amy Lei's students in their spectacular costumes performing traditional Chinese dances.

> "A RESEARCH TEAM DISCOVERED THAT BABIES AS YOUNG AS FIVE MONTHS OLD CAN DANCE!"

I thoroughly enjoyed writing about every dance for this book, and I hope you enjoy learning about them. If you start dancing in your classroom, blame the book!

Sharon Parsons

My sincere thanks to the following people for their time, information, images and enthusiasm for this book:

Amy Lei and students, Adelaide Chinese Dance Academy, Australia

AXIS Dance Company, California, the USA

Bangarra Dance Theatre, Sydney, Australia

Marcel Zentner, The University of York, the UK

AF746354

NELSON
CENGAGE Learning™
For learning solutions, visit **cengage.com.au**

Contents

Do You Want to DANCE?

1 Dance Crazes

Let's soft-shoe shuffle back in time to check out some popular dance crazes. **page 4**

2 Dance Choreographers

Who works out the steps and movements in a dance sequence? **page 9**

3 Do Babies Dance?

We humans move to music from a very early age. **page 12**

4 A Dance Company for All Abilities

Moving creatively to music is something everyone can enjoy. **page 13**

5 Aboriginal and Torres Strait Islander Dance

Dance can be a perfect way to pass on traditional stories. **page 14**

6 A Contemporary Aboriginal Dance Company

Combining old and new dance techniques can result in extraordinary performances.

page 16

7 Three Popular Classic Ballet Stories

Humour, tragedy, love, beauty and (sometimes) happy endings – ballet has it all!

page 18

8 Influential Dancers

Outstanding dancers have shaped their art form in ways that still influence contemporary dance.

page 22

9 Dance Sports

Being the best requires skill, talent, dedication – and lots of practice!

page 24

10 Chinese Dance School in Adelaide, Australia

Visit Amy Lei's dance school and see how her students excel in traditional Chinese dance.

page 28

Index and Glossary page 32

1 Dance Crazes

Imagine that you're relaxing in your bedroom listening to music. Think about which song would entice you to get up and start dancing. For many people in 1996 that song would be the macarena.

Macarena Dance Craze

The macarena was a very popular dance craze that began with a song called "Macarena" by a Spanish flamenco duo, Los del Rio. It was released in 1995, and became a hit in 1996. A flamenco dance teacher created the dance moves in 1996 and music videos helped to catapult the dance to fame in many countries around the world. The macarena became a dance craze because of its simple yet fun beat and Latin dance rhythm.

The single was the bestselling debut single of all time in the USA and, in 1996, about 50 000 people danced the macarena in New York City's Yankee Stadium.

Dance Moves for Macarena

The Macarena is a series of 16 dance moves that change with each beat.

Beat 1: Move your right arm straight out in front of you with your palm down.

Beat 2: Move your left arm straight out in front of you with your palm down.

Beat 3: Keeping your right arm straight in front of you, turn your palm up.

Beat 4: Keeping your left arm straight in front of you, turn your palm up.

Beat 5: Place your right hand on your left shoulder and hold.

Beat 6: Place your left hand on your right shoulder and hold (arms are criss-crossed).

Beat 7: Put your right hand behind your head.

Beat 8: Put your left hand behind your head.

Beat 9: Move your right hand across your body and place it on the front of your left hip.

Beat 10: Move your left hand across your body and place it on the front of your right hip.

Beat 11: Place your right hand on the right side of your bottom.

Beat 12: Place your left hand on the left side of your bottom.

Beat 13: Slightly rotate your hips to the left.

Beat 14: Slightly rotate your hips to the right.

Beat 15: Slightly rotate your hips to the left.

Beat 16: Clap your hands and jump while turning 90 degrees to your left. Repeat the sequence until the song has finished.

A Century of Dance Crazes – 1910s to 1990s

Now, let's soft-shoe shuffle back to some popular music and dance eras of the past hundred years – a period during which music technology advanced, resulting in cheaper and better-quality recordings and the widespread distribution of music, which made it more readily available.

1910s

The tango is a dance of Spanish-American origin and evolved in Argentina, South America. During the 1910s the tango quickly spread to other parts of the world. Its popularity was based on two elements: the dance style was radically different from anything that had gone before, as dance steps were improvised and it was performed by a couple facing each other. Since its beginning, many forms of tango have been created, each involving different techniques. The most popular styles of tango are the Argentine tango and Uruguayan tango.

1920s

The charleston was one of the most popular dances during the jazz era – the 1920s to the 1940s. The dance was created when a song of the same name was performed in a Broadway musical in New York, USA, in 1923.

playing jazz in the 1920s

dancing to jazz music in the 1920s

dancing the charleston in 1925

1930s and 1940s

In the 1930s and 1940s, swing dances originated in the USA and one of the most popular swing dances was called the jitterbug.

dancing the jitterbug in 1939

dancing the jitterbug in 1942

1950s

This decade saw the beginning of the rock'n'roll era, when African-American musicians were composing a new upbeat style of music alongside that of other American artists. Their music appealed to mainstream audiences of all colours at a time when racial tensions were running high. Influential artists of the time included Chuck Berry, who was one of the first black rock'n'roll performers popular with both black and white audiences, and Elvis Presley, who was a white performer whose style and music helped to bring the sound of black musicians to a broader audience.

the "King of Rock and Roll" Elvis Presley

the "King of Twist" Chubby Checker

1960s

American rock'n'roll music inspired others to build on the style, and pop music quickly spread globally. The British pop group the Beatles came to be known as one of the most successful and influential bands in the history of recorded music. One of the most popular dance crazes was the twist, first danced to Chubby Checker's song of the same name. He was called the "King of Twist".

1970s

Many dance crazes in this decade were line dances, such as the nutbush, which was danced along to "Nutbush City Limits", a song performed by Tina Turner in 1973. The disco dance craze began as another style of line dancing towards the end of the 1970s.

1980s

Michael Jackson (1958–2009) was influenced by famous dancers such as Fred Astaire and Gene Kelly. His video clips show him to have been an innovative dancer and choreographer. Perhaps his most memorable dance style was the moonwalk. Always an artist who wanted to create something new in each music video, he used magic effects to create the famous anti-gravity lean, showcased in his video clip for the song "Thriller". In this video, pegs rose up through the stage floor so that Michael Jackson and his dancers could click their heels onto the pegs, and lean forward.

a talented choreographer and dancer

Michael Jackson doin[g] his famous moonwal[k]

1990s

Like the macarena, the chicken dance was very popular in the 1990s at social gatherings, such as weddings and birthdays.

THE CHICKEN DANCE

This dance was first composed in Switzerland in the 1950s and it was originally known as the duck dance. Over the next 40 years it had several names before finally becoming known as the chicken dance and reaching the height of its popularity in the 1990s.

2 Dance Choreographers

Dancers Dance and Choreograph

A choreographer is someone who creates and arranges dance movements in a performance. A person with these skills often starts out as a dancer so has an understanding of the technical aspects of dance. As a choreographer, they may still dance professionally, and can also work for a dance company or have their own dance school.

The Silent Stars of Dance

Dance companies, dancers and audiences rely on a choreographer's ability to create memorable dance sequences. Ideally, a choreographer should have an excellent understanding of dance techniques, and an energetic inspiring personality to motivate dancers to perform at their very best. These people work behind the scenes, often for many months, to perfect dancers' techniques and movements during rehearsals and performances on stage.

Choreography in Conservative Times

The early 1900s was a conservative time for most young people who wanted to earn money as dancers or choreographers, and was especially tough for girls. Most parents would allow their kids to dance for fun but not earn a living from it.

Famous Choreographers: Martha and Agnes

Many accomplished dancers and choreographers of today draw inspiration from the stories of two American girls – Martha Graham (1894–1991) and Agnes de Mille (1905–1993). Martha and Agnes desperately wanted to become dancers despite their parents' disapproval. In their own unique ways, both girls managed to follow their dreams and become two of the most successful dancers of their time.

During their careers, they founded dance schools in New York, and became famous choreographers. Both Martha and Agnes worked at their dance schools until they died – Martha was 96 years old and Agnes was 88 years old.

Agnes and Martha were friends and often worked with many of the same people in dance. In 1991, Agnes de Mille published a biography about her friend, titled *Martha: The Life and Work of Martha Graham*.

Martha Graham with a dance partner

Martha's Inspiration to Dance

Martha was inspired to become a dancer when she saw dancer Ruth St Denis perform in 1914.

RUTH ST DENIS

Ruth St Denis (1880–1968) was one of the founders of modern dance in the USA. She danced in many Broadway musicals.

A First for Martha

Martha was the first dancer invited to dance at the White House, where she performed for President Franklin D. Roosevelt.

Hollywood Connections for Agnes

Agnes de Mille's uncle was famous Hollywood movie producer named Cecil de Mille. Her father, William de Mille, was a famous playwright, film producer and director. When Agnes was eleven years old, her father cast her in his 1916 movie, *The Ragamuffin*.

Agnes de Mille

Agnes' Inspiration to Dance

As a teenager, Agnes de Mille was inspired to dance when she saw a performance by the famous ballet dancer Anna Pavlova.

ANNA PAVLOVA

Anna Pavlova (1881–1931) was born in Russia and is considered to be the greatest ballet dancer of her time.

A First for Agnes

In 1943, Agnes became the first woman to work as a choreographer (then known as a dance director) on New York's famous Broadway.

BROADWAY

Broadway is a street in Manhattan, New York, famous for its theatres, where many plays and musicals are performed from Tuesday to Sunday every week, even on Christmas Day!

3 Do Babies Dance?

When babies hear music do they dance? A research team based at the prestigious University of York in the United Kingdom discovered that babies as young as five months old do dance!

Dance to the Beat!

The study, conducted by psychologist Marcel Zentner and his research team, observed 120 infants between the ages of five months and two years. As part of the experiment, the team filmed young children naturally moving their bodies to the rhythms of music.

Marcel Zentner

"I only dance to good music beats!"

Experiment Process

1. First, each baby's parent put on headphones so they couldn't hear the music. This was so they would not move to the beat of the music.
2. Once each baby was settled on their parent's lap, the researchers began playing recorded excerpts of classical music and rhythmic drumbeats. The babies' responses were filmed.
3. Then the research team played speech to the young ones. This was done as a control measure so that the researchers could compare the babies' rhythmic movements in relation to music and speech.
4. After the experiment, the research team worked with a team of ballet dancers to analyse how the babies and infants moved in time to the music.

The Experiment's Findings

The research team concluded that the infants moved parts of their bodies in time to the beat (not the melody) of different styles of music, but they didn't respond in the same way to speech. An even more important finding was that when the babies were able to move in time to the beat, they smiled!

4 A Dance Company for All Abilities

AXIS Dance Company is an innovative group of dancers with and without disabilities based in California, the USA. Since 1987, AXIS has created contemporary dances for stage performances that have captivated audiences throughout the world. Their dancers may have different physical abilities but they all share a talent for expressing themselves creatively through dance.

AXIS offers a vibrant program of dance activities for children in their "Dance Access/KIDS" classes. In the studio, children learn to collaborate as a team and create unique dances that cater to all physical abilities. To raise awareness in schools, the AXIS dancers make presentations to students about the dance company, the dancers and disability.

An AXIS dancer works in an elementary school in the USA.

AXIS dancers create dance forms that look like living sculptures.

AXIS

In dance, the term "axis" refers to the straight line or point around which a body or thing spins. At AXIS Dance Company, the thing that is spinning on an axis is usually a wheelchair.

5 Aboriginal and Torres Strait Islander Dance

In Australian Aboriginal and Torres Strait Islands culture, dance provides an important way of recording a rich history and tradition. In Aboriginal and Torres Strait Islander culture, people express themselves through dance in many kinds of traditional ceremonies.

Aboriginal Dreaming

In Aboriginal culture, the Dreaming is a collection of ideas, rituals and spiritual beliefs that links the past, present and future. It is expressed through stories of Aboriginal ancestors who moved across the lands to create life, the land and the laws. For thousands of years, the Dreaming has been passed between generations through dance, stories, songs and paintings.

Corroborees

The English word "corroboree", based on the Aboriginal word "caribberie", refers to a ceremonial gathering. These important occasions of dance and music are a traditional way for Aboriginal and Torres Strait Islander peoples to pass stories of the Dreaming from generation to generation and group to group. Communities have their own dances that tell their stories. Some are called:

- Joonba, which is a heritage corroboree
- Wangka, which is a celebratory or festive corroboree
- Munga Munga, which is a women's corroboree.

Torres Strait Islander Peoples' Dance

Communities in the Torres Strait Islands live near the sea and fishing is central to their livelihood. Their dances, costumes and musical instruments reflect their island environment and fishing culture. Instruments and headdresses are often made from shark teeth, skin and cartilage.

Different island groups have dances that refer to their specific surroundings. For example, in the Baizam (shark) dance from the island of Mer (Murray Island), one dari (headdress) worn by a dancer is made out of twine and banana leaves and has a carved wooden shark on top. A dari worn by another dancer is placed in the wooden shark's mouth.

The Torres Strait Islands Flag

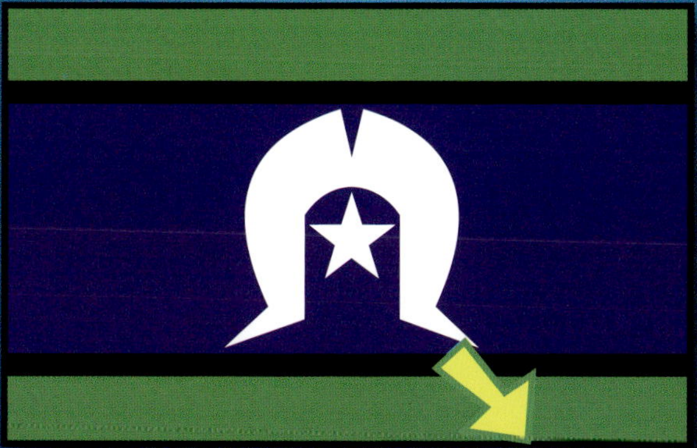

dancers from the group Nunukul Yuggera, one of Australia's best dance groups, performing in Brisbane, Queensland, during an Aboriginal festival

a young dancer wearing traditional costume, including the dari

6 A Contemporary Aboriginal Dance Company

bangarra

Bangarra Dance Theatre is Australia's most notable indigenous dance company. Established in 1989, Bangarra draws on over 60 000 years of Aboriginal culture translating the traditional stories, music and dance into contemporary theatrical experiences. The majority of staff at the Bangarra Dance Theatre have Aboriginal or Torres Strait Island heritage, and, led by Artistic Director Stephen Page, these talented indigenous storytellers are respectful of the past when creating unique and memorable dance productions that celebrate their people and cultures.

Bangarra Dance Theatre dancers

In Rites, *Bangarra created a unique dance production using the music of a Russian composer. The* Rites *performance was an Australian Ballet production in collaboration with Bangarra.*

Social Studies

Artistic Director, Stephen Page

Stephen Page is of Aboriginal descent – he describes his father as a freshwater man from Yugambeh tribe, Munaldjali clan, and his mother as a saltwater woman from the Nunukul, Ngugi mob, from Stradbroke Island, Queensland. After a successful dance journey with Sydney Dance Company and Aboriginal and Islander Dance Theatre (AIDT); he became the Artistic Director of Bangarra in 1991.

A Bangarra Choreographer

Frances Rings had a long career as a dancer before she began to choreograph. Since joining Bangarra Dance Theatre in 1993, she has choreographed several dance productions for the company. Frances is a descendant of the Kokatha tribe and has German heritage, too.

Frances Rings

a Bangarra choreographer and dancer in rehearsal for the dance Terrain

Bangarra's 2012 dance production, Terrain, *was inspired by the beauty and indigenous tradition associated with Lake Eyre. For tens of thousands of years the Aboriginal people lived in the Lake Eyre Basin and their stories reflect that close relationship with the landscape.*

The Lake Eyre Basin stretches across Queensland, South Australia, Western Australia and New South Wales. It covers about a sixth of Australia!

7 Three Popular Classic Ballet Stories

Classical ballet is a form of dance that can communicate complex and moving stories. Three of the world's most famous classical ballets, based on traditional European stories, have united dancers and audiences of many different cultures. These ballets are *The Nutcracker, The Sleeping Beauty* and *Swan Lake*.

The composer of these ballets, Pyotr Ilyich Tchaikovsky, and the choreographer, Marius Petipa, worked together to become one of the greatest composer-and-choreographer teams in ballet history.

Pyotr Tchaikovsky

Arts and History

Pyotr Tchaikovsky

Pyotr Ilyich Tchaikovsky (1840–1893) was a musical composer born in Russia. Although now regarded as one of the most respected musical storytellers ever, during his lifetime he achieved only limited success, as critics weren't ready for his open and emotional style of music. His music and his life story are an inspiration to creative composers today.

Marius Petipa

Arts and History

Marius Petipa

Marius Petipa (named at birth Victor Marius Alphonse Petipa) was born in France in 1818 and died in 1910. He was an accomplished French ballet dancer who became more famous in Russia both as a ballet dancer and then as a choreographer. He is renowned for being the inventor of modern classical ballet and produced more than 60 ballets in Russia.

Petipa's command of the Russian language wasn't very good, so his instructions to dancers on big productions, such as Swan Lake, were often something like "You on me", which meant that the dancer had to move from one corner ("You") to where he was standing ("Me").

The Most Performed Ballet Story: *The Nutcracker*

In 1891, Tchaikovsky composed the Nutcracker Suite and Petipa choreographed an accompanying ballet based on the story *The Nutcracker and the Mouse King* by ETA Hoffmann. Since the 1940s *The Nutcracker* has become the most performed ballet of all time. The story takes place on Christmas Eve and tells the story of a young German girl who has a dream at midnight about toys that come to life, a fierce battle and a prince who takes her to the Land of Snow and the Land of Sweets.

a scene from
The Nutcracker

A Timeless Ballet Story: *The Sleeping Beauty*

In 1889, Tchaikovsky composed the music for the ballet *The Sleeping Beauty*, which Petipa choreographed. It is Tchaikovsky's longest composition for ballet and lasts for almost four hours. (*Swan Lake* only lasts for about two hours.)

An eight-year-old Anna Pavlova was inspired to become a ballet dancer when she saw the ballet *The Sleeping Beauty*. (More about Anna Pavlova on page 11).

Anna Pavlova in 1916

A Tragic Love Story for Ballet: *Swan Lake*

Tchaikovsky composed the music for the ballet *Swan Lake* between 1875 and 1876. At the time, Tchaikovsky and Petipa did not work together on this production. However, after Tchaikovsky's death in 1893, Petipa choreographed a revised version of Tchaikovsky's *Swan Lake*, which was first performed in 1895 and has since become the best-known version.

a scene from Swan Lake

The ballet is a story of a prince, an evil sorcerer, and two sisters, Odette and Odile, who are turned into swans by the sorcerer. "The Flight of the Swans" is a famous musical piece that is danced by Odette and her maidens as swans. The same piece of music is cleverly re-introduced at a faster tempo in the fourth act to signal Odette and the prince's death in the lake. At the end of the ballet, the lake disappears and Odette and her prince re-emerge united.

8 Influential Dancers

In every country and culture, there are people who have a natural gift to express themselves in dance performances that are truly memorable. Their skill may not just be in their dance moves and techniques, but also in their ability to create a brand-new style of dance. Some of the memorable dancers who have come to the public's attention through their work in movies and theatre are featured in this chapter.

John Travolta

A research study in 2008 indicated that many people believed that the most memorable disco dancer was John Travolta (1954–) in the movie *Saturday Night Fever* (1977). John Travolta's dance performance for the song "Greased Lightning" in the popular movie *Grease*, made a year later, also rates highly among the most memorable of modern dances.

Katherine Dunham

Katherine Dunham (1909–2006) has been called "Dance's Katherine the Great", because she was one of the most influential and innovativ jazz dancers of her time.

Fred Astaire

Fred Astaire (1899–1987) was a great dancer and choreographer whose popularity on stage and screen rose in the 1930s and 1940s and peaked in the 1950s. His contribution to the arts endured for many years and he will be remembered for the poise, elegance and style that he brought to his dances, which included seemingly effortless tap-dancing sequences. As an actor and singer, he starred in more than 30 Hollywood movie musicals.

Rudolph Nureyev and Margot Fonteyn

Russian Rudolph Nureyev (1938–1993) is considered to have been the most influential and exceptional male ballet dancer of his time. He danced with many female ballet dancers but his partnership with the great ballet dancer Margot Fonteyn (1919–1991) is the most memorable for many people.

Rudolph Nureyev and Margot Fonteyn

9 Dance Sports

TEXT TYPE
Information Report
pages 24–27

There are millions of people around the world who compete in dance sport championships and competitions. Elite dance sport competitors undertake strength, endurance and cardiovascular training as well as lots of dancing practice. At an Olympic level, this translates to many hours of training a week. Dance sports at the Olympics include synchronised swimming, rhythmic gymnastics and figure skating. These sports all feature creative sequences using pre-determined movements in time to music.

A Demonstration Olympic Sport – Synchronised Skating

Synchronised skating is likened to theatre on ice. The sport made its debut as a demonstration sport at the Winter Olympics in 2002. In a demonstration sport, the athletes display their skills but do not compete for medals. Though synchronised skating is not yet a competitive Olympic event, there are World Synchronised Skating Championships held every year. This skilfully artistic sport continues to grow in popularity around the world.

Creativity on the Ice

Synchronised ice-skating team sizes can vary from eight to 30 skaters, depending on their division level. In competitive events, teams need to showcase their ice-skating skills as creatively choreographed sequences to music in a theatrical way. The challenge is heightened by the sport's strict rules (relating to the ice rink surface area, number of skaters in a team and program duration), and skaters must incorporate specific steps and movements into their routines.

Thematic Costumes

Costume designers create the outfits worn by the team members. These costumes factor in comfort and practicality but must also add to the "story" that the choreographed routine is telling. For example, champion Finnish synchronised ice-skating team Marigold IceUnity have skated wearing pirate costumes and false moustaches for a Captain Hook-themed routine.

TEXT TYPE
Information Report
pages 24–27

Olympic Sport – Synchronised Swimming

Synchronised swimming (often shortened to "synchro") is a sport that expects its competitors to be strong and fit, yet artistic and graceful, while coordinating their movements to music and holding their breath underwater. Synchronised swimmers combine the skills of swimming, gymnastics and dance with the aim of presenting perfectly timed artistic sequences in either a duet or a team. The swimmers are judged on the complexity of their sequences as well as how well they synchronise their movements as a team and with the music. Synchronised swimming movements all have names: "sailboat", "flamingo", "fishtail" and "knight" are all commonly used movements. The most important movement, one used to keep swimmers afloat while they move their arms above water, is called the "eggbeater".

in perfect formation

Sports

Specifications in the Pool

A synchronised swimming pool must have regulation specifications: area (20 metres wide by 30 metres long); temperature (26 degrees Celsius); performance area (12 metres by 12 metres and at least three metres deep); speakers (of a quality that enables the swimmers to hear their music).

Synchronised swimmers need to use special products for their make-up, hair and skin to maintain an appearance that aligns with regulations.

flowing rhythmic ribbon movements

Olympic Sport – Rhythmic Gymnastics

The sport of rhythmic gymnastics merges techniques of dance, gymnastics and ballet. There are individual and team-based events and the competitors perform on an area of floor that is 13 metres square. The competitors perform to the rhythm and beat of a musical piece, and can use one or two pieces of equipment, like ribbons, ropes, hoops or balls. The ribbon event is one of the most popular with spectators as it involves seamless, flowing movements with a six-metre-long ribbon. While competitors in rhythmic gymnastics are mostly women, more and more men are competing. Many male competitors choose to add elements of martial arts into their routines.

Rhythmic Gymnastics: Group Olympic Results in London 2012

Gold Medal:	Silver Medal:	Bronze Medal:
Russia	Belarus	Italy

competing in rhythmic gymnastics

latin dancing competitors

Dancing for Gold

Currently, more traditional dance sports are not part of the Olympics. However, almost every type of dance has competitions at an international level where the best dancers of that style meet to display their skills and strive to be the best at what they do. As with any sport, the level of expertise and commitment required to be the best make these worthy competitions for all involved.

10 Chinese Dance School in Adelaide, Australia

Amy Lei is a classically trained dancer from Beijing, China, who moved to Adelaide, Australia, with her family in 2007. Amy is an accomplished dancer and opened the Adelaide Chinese Dance Academy for students who range in age from two-and-a-half years old to adults.

Dance from Two Years Old

Rehearsals for the Yangge Dance

Language

Amy teaches in Mandarin when there are no equivalent English words for certain Chinese names and terms.

Rehearsals

Amy's student do exercises that resemble ballet, and many that involve more athletic movements, such as cartwheels and back flips.

Dance and Culture

Amy integrates Chinese culture into her lessons so that her students understand the historical importance of each dance. One example is the Yangge dance performed by the Han ethnic group in Northern China. It is a festive dance performed by the Han ethnic group (China's main ethnic group) at celebrations, such as the Chinese New Year.

The Yangge Dance Performance

Music

Amy selects and edits the music for each dance.

Rehearsals for the Peacock Dance

> I CHOREOGRAPH ORIGINAL DANCES AND ADAPT OTHER WELL-KNOWN ONES.
>
> AMY LEI

The Peacock Princess

Yang Liping (1958–) is one of China's most famous folk dancers. People have known her as the "Peacock Princess" since 1986, when she performed the peacock dance at a national contest. Since that time, Yang has created a signature appearance that is inspired by the graceful features of a peacock, such as elegant costumes and long manicured nails.

Yang has long been inspired by the natural beauty of plant and animal life found in the Yunnan Province in China, and chooses to only portray nature in her dances. In 2012, she performed at a spring festival evening gala folk dance, called "Love of Peacocks".

At Yang's dance school in Yunnan Province, she gains pleasure from teaching folk dance to students who are just like she was – young children from poor families in villages.

Performances

Each year, Amy's students dance in more than ten major performances that reflect certain special days, like Chinese New Year, Moon Lantern Festival and Australia Day.

> I LOVE TO TEACH CHINESE DANCE; IT IS ALWAYS IN MY DREAMS WHEN I GO TO SLEEP.
>
> AMY LEI

The Peacock Dance Performance

Students perform the traditional Peacock Dance of the Dai people of Southern China.

Index

Aboriginal dance 14–17
babies 12
ballet 11, 18–21, 23
Bangarra 16–17
Chinese dance 28–31
choreographer 8–11, 13, 17, 18, 23
dance sport 24–27
Hollywood 11, 23
jazz 6, 22
macarena 4, 8
pop music 7
rock'n'roll 7
swing 6
tango 5
Torres Strait Islander dance 15

Glossary

Broadway The theatre district of New York, USA, famous for its many plays and dance performances

choreographer A person who creates and arranges dance movements in a performance

corroboree A ceremonial gathering of Aboriginal dance and music

craze Something that is popular for a short period of time

elite The best or most skilled members of a group

jazz A style of popular music with a forceful rhythm

rhythmic A piece of music or dance that has a regular beat

sequence In dancing, the order and arrangement of dance moves

swing A style of rhythmic dancing, first performed by jazz big bands in the 1930s

synchronised Action or movement that happens at exactly the same moment; operating in unison